Produced by
Allegra Publishing Ltd London
for Caxton Publishing Group

Editor : Felicia Law
Designer : Karen Radford

Published by
Mercury Junior an imprint of Mercury Books

20 Bloomsbury Street

London WC1B 3JH, UK

ISBN 9781845600426

The Three Pirates
Pirate Gold

Sheila McCullagh
Illustrated by Rupert van Wyk

Mercury Junior
20 Bloomsbury St, London, WC1B 3JH, UK

Once upon a time, there were three pirates.
Their names were Roderick, Greg and Ben.

Roderick had a black sack full of gold, and Greg had
a black sack full of gold. Ben had a big sack full of gold
too, but Ben's sack was blue.

(The pirates all wanted to hide their sacks of gold,
so that no other pirate would find them.)

Roderick had a brown
ship with red sails,
so he was called
Roderick the Red pirate.

Greg had a brown ship with green sails, and so he was called Greg the Green pirate. (Sometimes he was just called Greg the Green, for Greg was a bit of a fool. He was green in more ways than one!)

Ben had a brown ship too, but his sails were blue, so he was called Ben the Blue pirate.

They sailed their ships over the blue sea, looking for islands where they could hide their gold.

9

Roderick the Red pirate saw a little island.
There was a big rock in the sea by the island.

"Ah!" said Roderick. "I will hide my gold here and
no one will find it."

He took his sack of gold and went on to the island.
The wind blew his hat off on to the grass, but Roderick
didn't think about his hat. He was only thinking about
his gold. (Roderick was a very greedy pirate!)

He hid his sack of gold under a rock and went
back to his ship. And then he sailed
away on the sea.

Roderick was glad that his gold was well hidden – but he hadn't seen Greg's ship sailing towards the island!

Greg the Green pirate was looking for an island, when he saw the big rock in the sea.

"If I hide my gold on that island," Greg said to himself, "I can find the island again. I shall look for the big rock in the sea."

So he took his sack of gold and hid it on the island.

12

As he went back to the ship, Greg dropped his knife. He didn't see his knife drop so he didn't know he'd lost it. He sailed away on the sea and left his knife there on the island. (Greg often lost things. He even lost his way, as he sailed on the sea.)

Greg was glad that his gold was well hidden – but he hadn't seen Ben's ship sailing towards the island!

Ben sailed his ship till he came to the island. He saw Roderick's ship far away and he saw Greg's ship near the island, so he hid his ship in a cove until Greg had gone. Then he went on the island.

The sand was wet, so he took off his boots and left them on the sand by a rock.

He hid his gold under a tree on the island, and then he sailed away in his ship.

14

Greg forgot that he had left his knife on the island.

Roderick forgot that he had left his hat on the island.

But Ben stubbed his toe on the deck and it hurt.

"Ouch!" he said. "I've left my boots on that island.
I must have my boots. I'll go and find them where
I left them on the sand."

So he sailed back to the island to look for his boots.

The sky was blue and the sea was blue, and Ben
sang as he sailed his ship back to the island.

He left the ship by the big rock in the sea.
He went on to the island to look for his boots.

The island lay green and brown in the sunshine.
The sun shone on the flowers, and the sun shone
on the grass. The sun shone on the trees, and the
sun shone on the blue sea.

Ben saw his boots there by a rock.

"Oh good! My boots!" he said. He sat down and put them on and he went on over the sand.

But then, Ben saw the green pirate's knife lying in front of him.

"I know that knife," Ben said to himself.
"It belongs to Greg the Green pirate. Greg must have been on the island. That's not so good."
He picked up the knife.

Then he saw the red pirate's hat on the grass.
"So the red pirate has been on this island too,"
Ben said to himself. "That's very bad. I must hide
my gold on another island, where no other pirates
come. But first I will play a trick on the green
pirate and the red pirate." And, very carefully,
he hid Greg's knife under Roderick's hat.
"That will give them a surprise," he said.

Then Ben went on to look for his own gold.

He went this way and he went that way.

He looked this way and he looked that way.

His sack was hidden under a tree. Ben saw the tree and
took out his sack. He poured the gold out on the grass.
It shone in the sunshine. It was all there.

"So my gold is safe," Ben said to himself.
"But if the other pirates come back, they'll steal it."

So he put the gold back in the sack and took the
sack back to his ship. Then he sailed away on the sea.

The sun shone down on the blue sea and it was
very hot. Roderick the Red pirate was very hot too.
He had no hat and he got hotter and hotter.
He was so hot that he was purple.

And still the sun shone down.

Roderick puffed and he
puffed and he blew.
Then Roderick said to
himself as he puffed
and puffed and blew,

"There must be seas
and islands where it
is not so hot. I must
go back and find my
gold and hide it on
an island where it is
not so hot."

So Roderick sailed back to the
island by the big rock.

Roderick left his ship by the rock, and went on to the
island where he had hidden his gold.

The island lay green and brown in the sunshine. There
were blue flowers and white flowers in the grass, but
Roderick didn't see the flowers. Roderick never looked
at flowers.

Roderick went on over the island. He looked this way
and he looked that way and at last he saw the rock
where his gold lay hidden.

He went to the rock and took hold of his sack.
He took hold of the sack and he pulled hard.
But the sack was stuck fast under the rock.
"Come out!" shouted Roderick.

He pulled and he pulled and he PULLED, and the sack
came out in a rush. Roderick sat down hard with the
sack on top of him. He sat down VERY HARD INDEED!

"Oh!" said Roderick loudly. "Oh! Oh! Oh!
Blow!" said Roderick. "Blow! Blow! Blow!"

(He said "BLOW!" very loudly indeed.)

Then he got to his feet. "That was hot work
in the hot sun," he said. "I do need my hat."

Roderick looked around and at last he saw his hat.

"Ah!" he puffed, "that's my hat". But when he picked
it up, he saw Greg's knife! "That knife belongs to the
green pirate," he muttered. "What is it doing here?
Greg has been on this island! Perhaps his gold
is here! I will look for HIS gold too."

So Roderick looked under the rocks and under the trees,

and soon he saw the green pirate's sack under a rock.

He took hold of the sack and he pulled.

He didn't pull hard, but this time the sack came out.

He picked up the sack and shook it.

The gold fell on the grass and shone in the sunshine.

Roderick picked up the gold bit by bit.

He counted it as he went on. His eyes shone with greed.

He put Greg's gold in his own sack, with his own gold.
(Pirates always steal gold if they can get away with it.)

"And I'll steal his knife, too," said Roderick.
He laid the knife in the sack with all the gold.

Then he set off back to his ship feeling very pleased
with himself. But now the bag of gold was too heavy
to lift. It was so heavy that Roderick had to bump it
over the sand.

High in the sky, there was a little black cloud. But Roderick didn't see the cloud. He didn't look. He didn't feel the rain begin to fall. He didn't feel the sack get wet. He puffed and he pulled, and he pulled and he puffed.

And he didn't see that the
knife bumped down and down in the
sack, and cut a small slit in the side. Roderick
bumped on over the sand to his ship. The sack
grew wetter and wetter, and the slit grew bigger
and bigger, and the gold fell out bit by bit.
And Roderick didn't know!

29

Poor Roderick! He was such a greedy pirate and he
had lost most of his gold on the sand.
All he had left was a very wet, very heavy sack!

But Roderick didn't know. He pulled his sack on to his
ship, and sailed away. And as he sailed, he sang his
special song.

30

Roderick's song

Greg the Green pirate sailed away from the island, and sailed for a day across the sea. But as he went, he got tangled in a rope. He looked for his knife to cut the rope, but it wasn't there.

"Blow!" said Greg. "I must have left my knife on the island."

So he sailed his ship back to the rock.

Then he went on the island and looked for his knife.

He went this way and he went that way, but he couldn't

see his knife anywhere.

"Someone has taken my knife!" said Greg. "Perhaps the

red pirate has been on the island. Perhaps he has found

my knife. Blow! Perhaps he has even found my gold!"

So Greg went to look for his gold. He looked under this

rock and he looked under that rock, but he couldn't

see his gold.

The sun shone down and it was very hot.

The sunshine was hot and the sand was hot,

and Greg the Green pirate was very hot indeed.

He went this way and he went that way,

and at last he came to the sea again.

He fell over a stone and sat down hard on the sand.

"Oh!" cried Greg. "Oh! Ouch! Oh!"

But as he cried out, he looked up and saw a cliff.

There was a cave in the cliff!

"A cave!" cried Greg. "There's a cave in the cliff!
Pirates hide their gold in caves! Perhaps the red pirate
hid my gold there – and perhaps his gold is there too!"

Greg scrambled to his feet and went into the cave.
It was dark in the cave after the sunshine.
Greg didn't see the pit just inside the cave and he fell
into the pit with a bang – CRASH!

"Oh!" cried Greg. "Oh! Ouch! Oh! Ouch!"

But he didn't say "Oh" very loudly: there was too much
sand in his mouth.

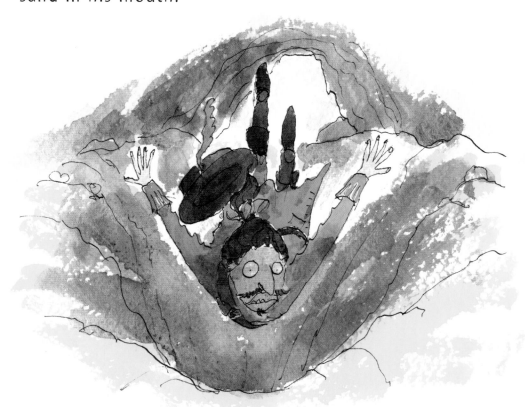

Greg spat out the sand and sat up. But as he tried to get up, more sand fell in and he banged his toe on something hard. The sand fell on his face and it fell on his feet, and a stone fell on his head too. Greg spat the sand out again and sat up. But when he tried to get up, more sand fell in.

Greg sat down again hard. He sat down very hard.

"Oh!" cried Greg, "it's very hard! It's very hard on me!
I've fallen in and I can't get out. It's very hard indeed!"

He put his hand down to rub himself and he felt
something hard, very, very hard and it wasn't a stone!

Greg forgot about the bump on his head. He forgot about the pain in his toe. He turned himself around in the hole and looked. He was sitting on a wooden chest.

"A chest!" cried Greg. "A pirate's treasure chest! Some pirate has hidden his treasure here!"

He struggled to his feet and picked up the stone and banged the lock in the lid of the chest. The chest fell open. It was full of jewels. There were red rubies and green emeralds and blue sapphires in the chest.

"Treasure!" cried Greg. "Rubies! Emeralds! Sapphires!"

Greg tried to pick
up the chest but it
was stuck in the hole.
He pulled and he pulled
and he PULLED. But the
chest was stuck fast.
It would NOT come out.
So Greg filled his pockets
with the jewels. He filled
his pockets with rubies and
emeralds and sapphires.
He shut the lid of the treasure
chest and stood on the lid.
And one way and another,
he pulled himself out.
(He only fell back once.)

Greg went back along the sands until he saw the big rock in the sea, and then he saw his ship near the island. So Greg went back to his ship with his pockets full of jewels, and a bump on his head and a bump on his toe. "But still I haven't got my sack of gold," Greg said to himself. "And that's very hard. That's very, very hard on me! I shall have to sail away, day after day, to find my sack of gold!"

So Greg sailed away from the island in his ship. He was glad he had the jewels, but he wasn't very happy. He still wanted his sack of gold. Greg found it hard to be happy. So as he sat on his ship, he sang a song, and this is what he sang:

Greg's song

Sing in a worried voice

Ben the Blue pirate was sailing too. He sat on his ship and the ship sailed over the blue sea.

"I must sail away and find another island," Ben said to himself, "an island where other pirates will never come. Far away across the sea, there is an island, the island of Acrooacree."

And Ben sat on his ship and he sang:

Ben's song

Sing with an easy lazy voice

And as he sailed, the sun went down and the red in the sky shone red in the sea. Ben went to his cabin to sleep.

And far away, very far away the storm wind sang.

And another adventure was about to begin!

Will Ben reach his dream island of Acrooacree?

Will Greg find his missing gold — which Roderick

has stolen?

And will Roderick find out that the stolen gold

fell out of his sack?

If you have enjoyed this story,

there are many more adventures of

The Three Pirates.